# BISCUIT Bear

## MINi GReY

JONATHAN CAPE
London

**Our story** starts with a lump of pastry that Horace's Mum gave him, which Horace would usually roll about over the floor and furniture

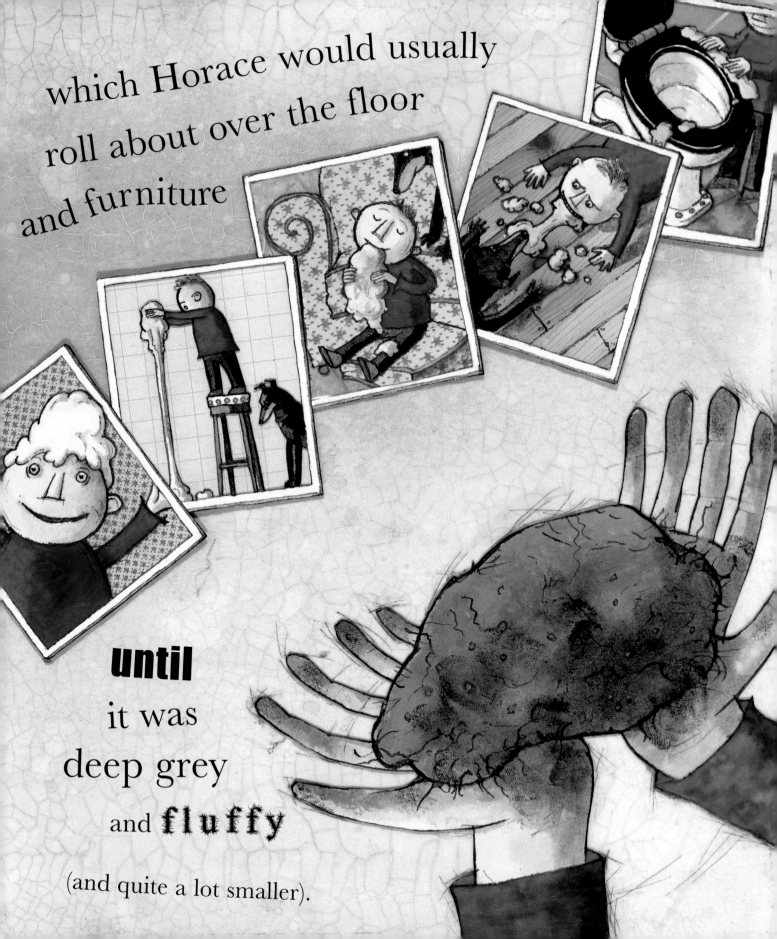

until
it was
deep grey
and **fluffy**

(and quite a lot smaller).

**But today**

Horace's Mum gave him
a biscuit cutter in the shape of
a bear to use.

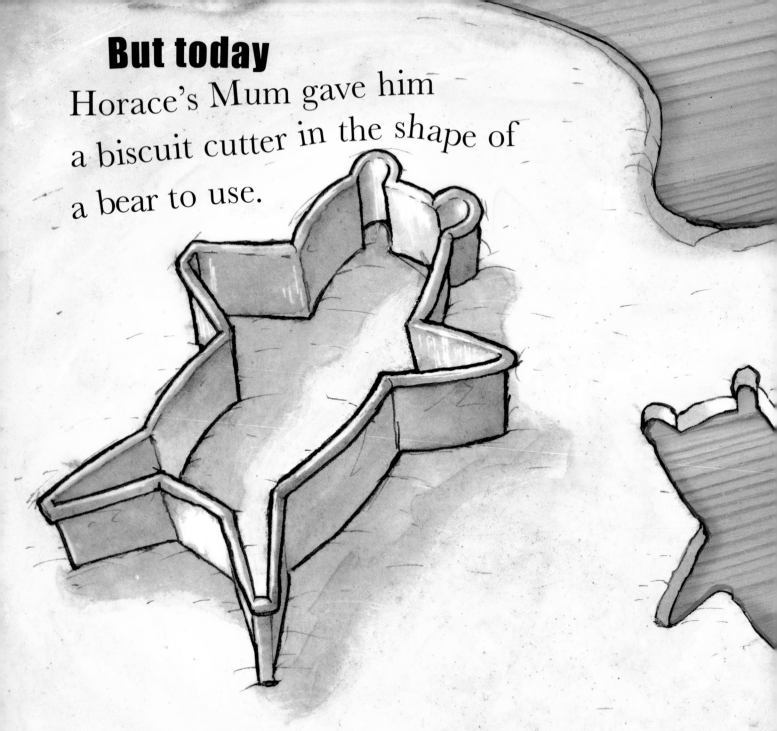

Horace stamped out a pastry bear
and gave it currant eyes and a nose.

Horace's Mum put it in the oven to cook.

**Twenty minutes** later the biscuit bear was golden-coloured and smelt lovely, and Horace wanted to take a bite *but –*

**"No, Horace,"** said Horace's Mum, "it is too hot. You must wait for it to cool down."

**An hour** later Horace remembered the cooled biscuit bear and was about to take a bite *but –*

**Before bedtime**
Horace thought of the golden biscuit bear and he was just gazing at it, but –

**"No, Horace,"**

said Horace's Mum,
"you have just cleaned your teeth."

**"No, Horace,"**

said Horace's Mum,
"you are just about to have dinner. You will spoil your appetite."

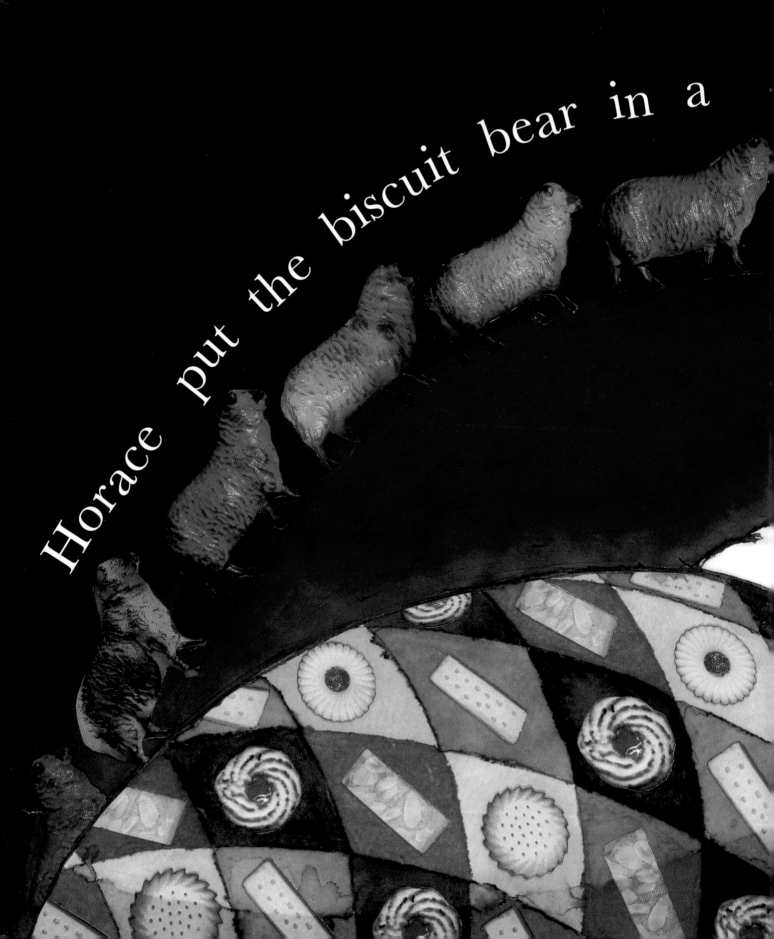

Horace put the biscuit bear in a

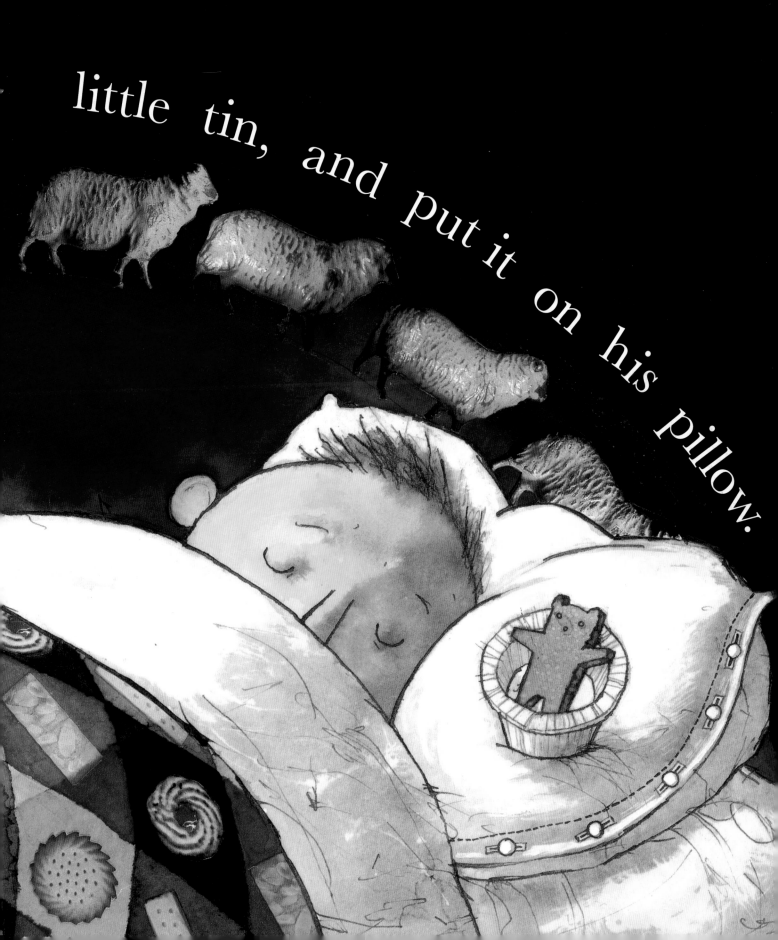

little tin, and put it on his pillow.

It was the
**middle of the night.**
Biscuit Bear woke up.
He yawned and stretched,
and looked about for
somebody to play with.
Everyone seemed
to be asleep.

Biscuit Bear had an idea.
I shall **make** some friends,
he said to himself,
and went to the **kitchen**.

Biscuit Bear found  **butter** and **flour** and **milk.**

He **mixed** up a mixture,
and **rolled** it
and **shaped** it,

and put the first batch of friends in the oven to cook.

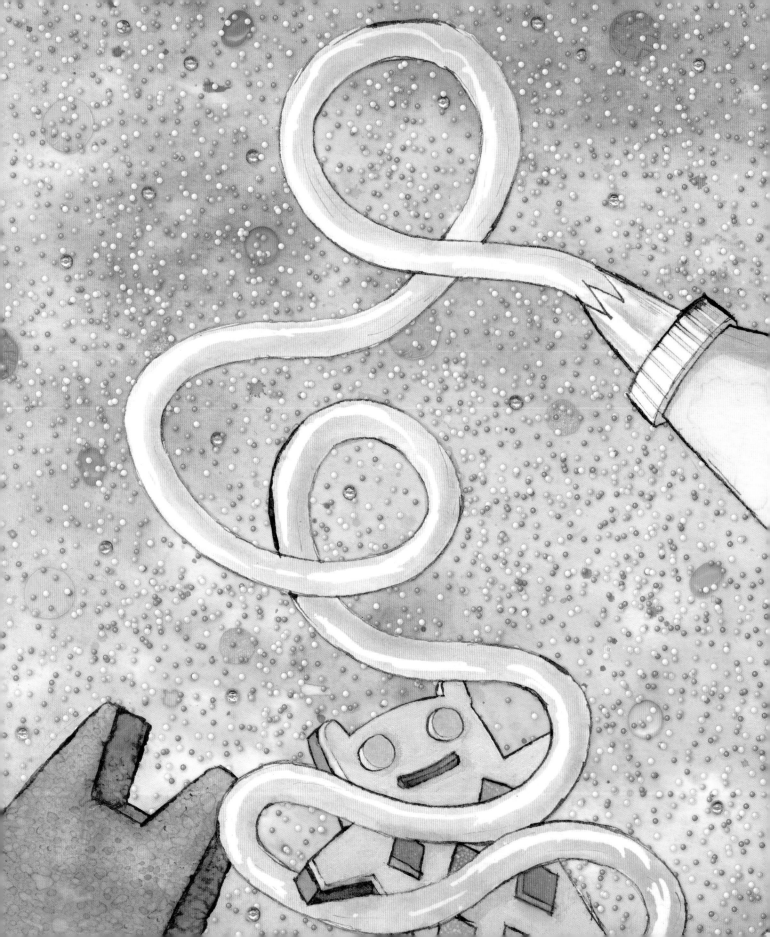

When they had cooled,
Biscuit Bear dressed them in
*icing* of many colours,
hundreds and thousands,
and **candied peel** and **glacé** cherries
and little silver balls.

"And now,"
Biscuit Bear said
to his new friends,
"let the fun begin!"

# Roll Up!
# Roll Up!

One night only!
Biscuit Bear's Circus is
performing in
the kitchen!

**Watch** the Acrobats
as they
toss and tumble!

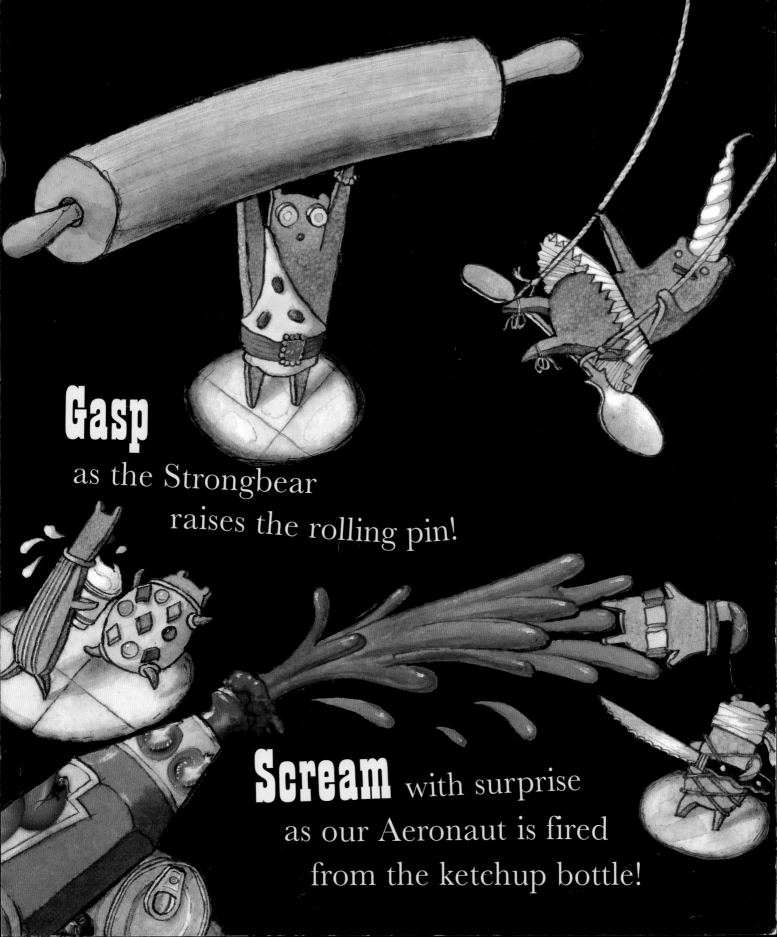

**Gasp**
as the Strongbear
raises the rolling pin!

**Scream** with surprise
as our Aeronaut is fired
from the ketchup bottle!

The circus was so exciting
that no one noticed
the **shadow** looming
in the doorway.

**Bongo the Dog** liked biscuits.
(But not in a way that is
necessarily good
for the
biscuits.)

Biscuit Bear **just** managed to clamber to safety.

Biscuit Bear looked sadly at the mess.
He suddenly realized
that he needed to find
a place where a biscuit
could be safe.

When Horace awoke the **next morning,**
he reached for the tin
that had contained the little biscuit bear,

but all he found was crumbs,
and a card
that looked
familiar.

The life of a biscuit
is usually **short** and *sweet,*
but Biscuit Bear has found
somewhere safe to be.

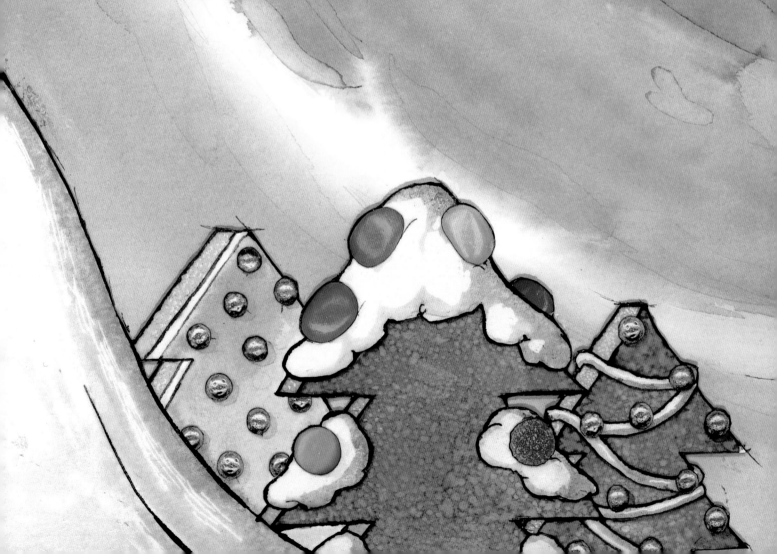

Biscuit Bear is in
the Pastry Shop Display.
Some of it is cardboard,
covered in icing;
some of it is plaster –
it looks delicious,
but it can never be eaten.

The display changes
through the
year –

but Biscuit Bear is
always the **star;**
spring, summer
and winter.

*Dedicated to*

# Jo

(and to biscuit lovers everywhere)

BISCUIT BEAR
A JONATHAN CAPE BOOK 0 224 06496 7

Published in Great Britain by Jonathan Cape,
an imprint of Random House Children's Books

This edition published 2004

1 3 5 7 9 10 8 6 4 2

RANDOM HOUSE CHILDREN'S BOOKS
61–63 Uxbridge Road, London W5 5SA
A division of The Random House Group Ltd

RANDOM HOUSE AUSTRALIA (PTY) LTD
20 Alfred Street, Milsons Point, Sydney,
New South Wales 2061, Australia

RANDOM HOUSE NEW ZEALAND LTD
18 Poland Road, Glenfield, Auckland 10, New Zealand

RANDOM HOUSE (PTY) LTD
Endulini, 5A Jubilee Road, Parktown 2193, South Africa

THE RANDOM HOUSE GROUP Limited Reg. No. 954009
www.**kids**at**r**andomhouse.co.uk

A CIP catalogue record for this book is available from the British Library.

Printed in Singapore

DISCARD